Thelma THE Unicorn

AARON BLABEY

SCHOLASTIC

Thelma felt a little sad.
In fact, she felt forlorn.
You see, she wished with all her heart
to be a unicorn.

Her best friend's name was Otis.
He liked her quite a lot.
He said, 'You're perfect as you are.'

But Thelma said, 'I'm not.'

And that was when she saw it.
A carrot on the ground.
It gave her such a great idea,
she squealed and jumped around.

She took that simple carrot
and she tied it to her nose.
'I'll SAY that I'm a unicorn!
It might just work . . .
who knows?'

Well, as she did, a truck drove by.
The driver rubbed his eyes.
'Good grief! Is that a unicorn?!'
he shrieked in great surprise.

As Thelma watched the swerving truck,
it very nearly hit her.
Would you believe that truck was filled
with nice pink paint and glitter?

Oh, Thelma looked amazing!
She WAS a unicorn.

'I'm *special* now!'

she cried out loud.

And so a star was born . . .

All across the whole wide world
her fans would cheer her name.

Thelma loved it! Every bit!
The FAME!
The FAME!
The FAME!

Thelma was a superstar!
Her dreams had all come true.

The Fairy Princess

But soon she found that so much fame
was kind of tricky too . . .

You see, her fans were mad for her.
They'd scream and cry and laugh.
They'd chase her everywhere she went
to get her autograph.

In fact, they'd chase her all day long.

It NEVER

EVER stopped.

They chased her while she exercised.

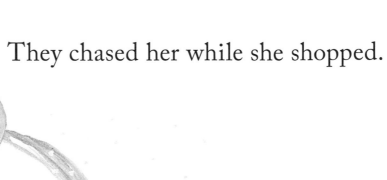

They chased her while she shopped.

'Please don't chase me anymore,'
she asked the screaming crowd.
'We'll chase you all we want,' they said.
'We're fans, so it's allowed!'

And some were not her fans at all.
No, some were really mean.

And some just did the meanest things
she'd really ever seen.

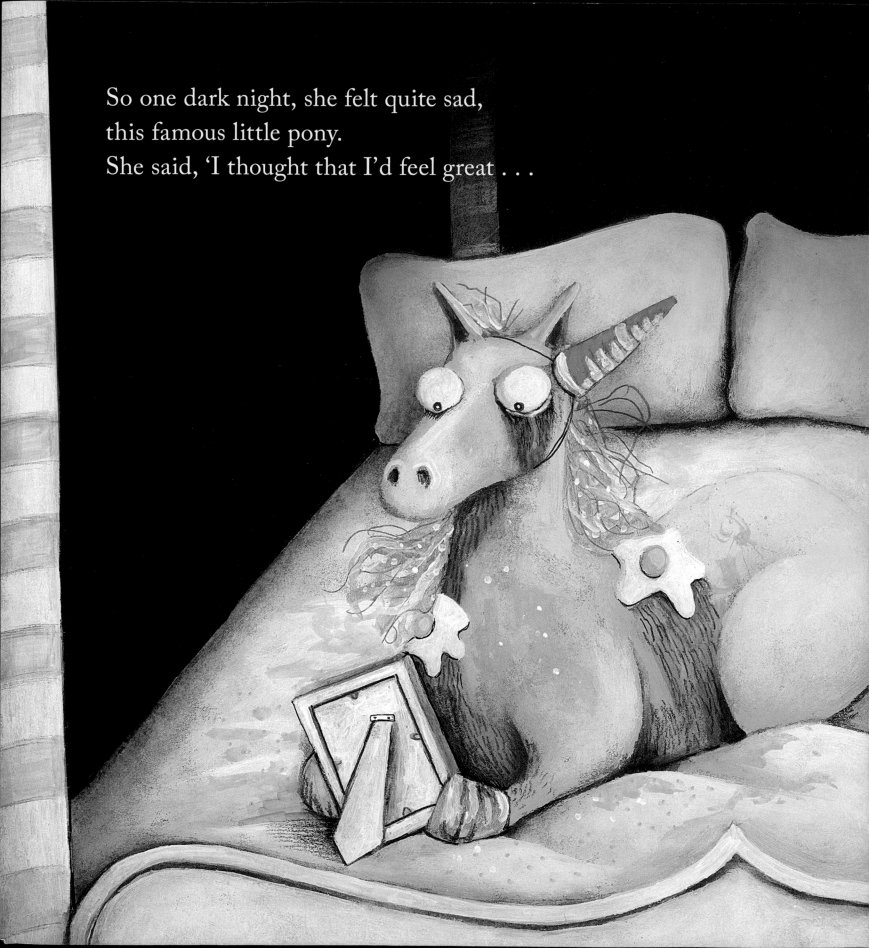

So one dark night, she felt quite sad,
this famous little pony.
She said, 'I thought that I'd feel great . . .

. . . but all I feel is lonely.'

And so with that
she changed her mind,
this lonely unicorn.

She cleaned off
all her sparkles.

And she ditched her magic horn.

And then she walked right past the crowd.
They didn't even notice.

She thought how nice that it would be . . .

. . . to see her lovely Otis.

And when he asked about her trip,
beneath their favourite tree,
she simply said, 'Oh, it was fun . . .

. . . but I'd rather just be me.'